SODY SALLYRATUS

retold by Joanne Compton
illustrated by Kenn Compton

Holiday House/New York

For the schoolchildren of North Carolina, who are keeping the art of storytelling alive, and especially for all my first graders, past and present, who help me keep my stories alive.

—Joanne Compton

For Murray Craven—a good friend.
—Kenn Compton

Library of Congress Cataloging-in-Publication Data
Compton, Joanne.
Sody Sallyratus / retold by Joanne Compton ; illustrated by Kenn
Compton. — 1st ed.
p.   cm.
Summary : When Ma runs out of baking soda for her biscuits, two of
her sons and Ma herself disappear on the way to the store, leaving
her son Jack to solve the mystery.
ISBN 0-8234-1165-6
[1. Folklore — United States.]   I. Compton, Kenn, ill.   II. Title.
PZ8.1.C7353So   1995   94-28261   CIP   AC
398.2'097302 — dc20
[E]

AUTHOR'S NOTE

Folktales are exciting stories because they are alive—still being told and retold, generation after generation, and still being changed as storytellers add or subtract details and dialogue to suit their audiences. We knew the story of "Sody Sallyratus" from Richard Chase's version that he had collected and himself embellished in *Grandfather Tales* (Houghton Mifflin, 1948). The unusual title of the story is explained by Chase in *Grandfather Tales*. During the early days of American history, baking soda was called *saleratus*.

When we decided to retell "Sody Sallyratus," we researched the story and found many parallel elements in "The Greedy Old Fat Man," a West Virginia folktale, and in older tales such as "The Three Billy Goats Gruff," "The Johnny Cake," and "The Gingerbread Man." At the time we were pondering different versions of the story and practicing ways we might retell it, we visited North Carolina schoolchildren and talked about our first Jack tale, "Jack the Giant Chaser." Before we knew it, Jack had wandered into "Sody Sallyratus" and soon replaced the squirrel of Chase's version as the hero of the story. Jack's mother and two brothers were to replace Chase's other human characters, but that bothersome bear remained. The history of the story is not complete—it is now passed on to you, the reader.

—*Joanne Compton*

One fine morning, when Jack was on his way from here to there, he decided to stop by his ma's cabin and visit a bit with her and his two brothers, Tom and Will. They were all mighty glad to see Jack, and as soon as the howdy-dos were over, Ma went into the kitchen to make some biscuits for breakfast.

The boys sat on the front porch, and Jack began telling them of his adventures with the giant. All of a sudden, they heard an awful racket coming from the kitchen.

"Land's sake!" hollered Ma. "I done run out of sody sallyratus and without my sody sallyratus, I can't be baking biscuits!"

She looked out on the porch and saw those three boys sitting there.

"Tom, get yourself down to the store and fetch me back some sody sallyratus. And don't you be dawdling in the creek looking for crawdads."

"Don't you worry, Ma," said Tom. "I'll be back up 'fore the dew's dry on the laurel."

Off Tom ran, down the crooked path to get some sody sallyratus. The path twisted over the ridge and hung onto the steep side of the mountain. After a bit, Tom could hear the sound of Cold Water Creek, and he knew he was getting close to the old rickety footbridge that crossed over the water.

Just as Tom started to tramp across the bridge, up reared the biggest, ugliest bear he had ever laid eyes on.

"Ha!" growled the bear. "Here comes my breakfast, tramping across the bridge!" And before Tom could blink an eye, the bear gobbled him up.

Back at the cabin, Ma decided to come out on the porch to hear about Jack's adventures. The morning slipped away as Jack told her and Will about all he had seen and done since his last visit. Eventually, Ma went to the edge of the mountain and peered across the ridge.

"Now where is that Tom?" she exclaimed. "I jes' bet he's down by the creek messing with them crawdads. Will, you run on down there and fetch back that worthless boy and my sody."

"Don't worry, Ma," said Will, "I'll be back 'fore the sun crosses the high ridge."

And off Will ran, down the crooked path to find Tom and the sody sallyratus. It wasn't long before he was crossing the rickety old footbridge over Cold Water Creek. Suddenly, there was a great roar from underneath and then Will was standing face to face with the bear.

"Ha!" growled the bear. "Here comes my dinner, tramping across the bridge!"

And with that he gobbled Will up.

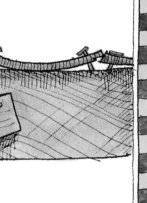

Back at the cabin, Jack helped his ma with her chores. While they worked, they talked of this and that. The sun climbed higher and higher in the sky, but Tom and Will still weren't back with the sody sallyratus.

"Them boys are both as useless as they come," muttered Ma. "Why I bother sending them to do anything at all is a wonder to me. Jack, you jes' set yourself down and rest a bit. I'm going to find them boys and my box of sody and drag 'em all three up here. I'll be back before dark falls."

Off Ma went down the crooked path to find Tom, Will, and the sody sallyratus. As she stomped across the rickety old footbridge over Cold Water Creek, the bear sprang up in front of her.

"HA!" growled the bear. "Here comes my supper, stomping across the bridge."

And he gobbled Ma up.

Back at the cabin, Jack waited around and waited around until he couldn't wait any longer.

"Something 'bout this ain't right," he said to himself. "I reckon I'm going to have to go down the mountain and see what's keeping everybody."

So Jack went down the crooked path to look for his ma and Will and Tom and the sody sallyratus. "Maybe I'll run into them on their way back up," he mumbled.

Pretty soon he was trotting across the rickety old footbridge.

Just like before, the bear popped up from under the bridge.

"Ha!" he laughed. "Here's me another little bite to eat!"

"Hold on there, friend," hollered Jack. "Have you seen my ma and my brothers come by here?"

"Sure I seen 'em," growled the bear. "They came stomping across my bridge, disturbing my sleep, so I gobbled 'em up and I is gonna gobble you up, too!"

The bear opened his jaws as wide as he could and edged closer to Jack.

"Well, friend, you're gonna have to catch me first!" Jack yelled as he ran back up the path and shinnied up the first tree he came to.

Jack has always been a quick sort of fellow, and he climbed as fast as he could, jumping from branch to branch. But when he looked down, the bear was close behind him.

Jack climbed and climbed until his head popped out into the sky. He had run out of tree.

That big old bear got closer and closer to the top, and as he did the tree began to lean more and more to one side. In fact it was almost touching the ground.

When the bear finally poked through the last branches, he saw Jack standing just a few feet off the ground.

"It won't do you no good to jump down, boy," chortled the bear. "I'll jes' come after you. If you'd stand still and let me eat you now, it'd save us both a lot of trouble."

"Well," said Jack, "you're probably right. You might as well come on and get it over with."

The bear crawled out onto the end of the tree toward Jack and opened his jaws as wide as he could. Just as he slammed them shut, Jack jumped down.

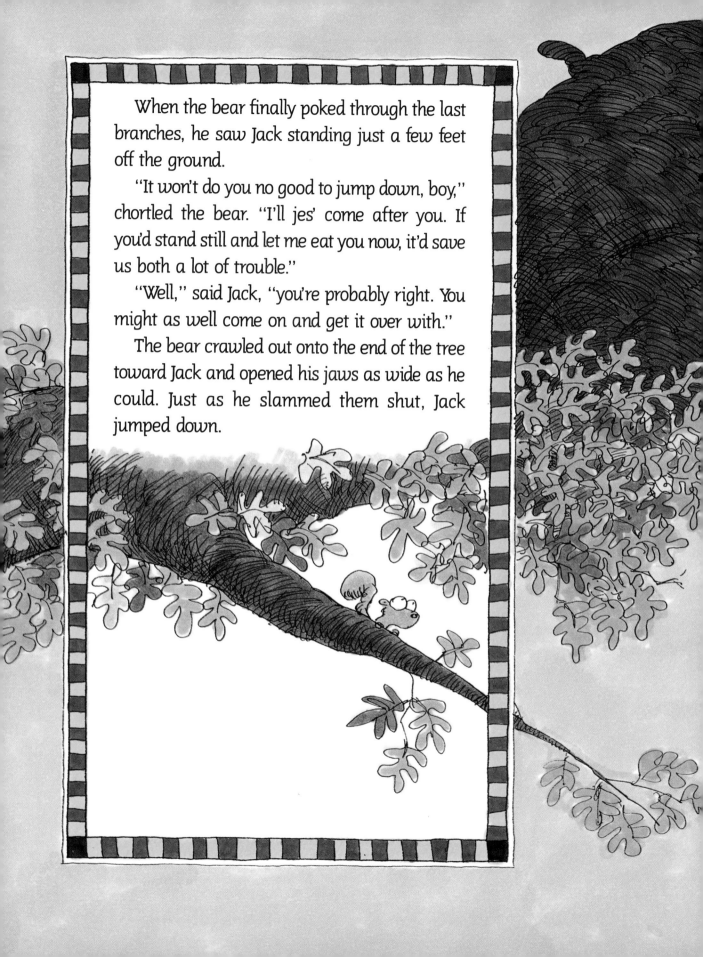

The tree twitched and trembled and then sprang straight up, flinging the bear out of its branches, over the treetops, and across Cold Water Creek.

The bear hit the ground so hard that Tom and Will and Jack's ma popped right out, safe and sound.

"WHOO-EE!" Ma shouted to Jack. "Me and the boys jes' had us some kind of adventure!"

"Let's go on home, and you can tell me all about it," laughed Jack.

So Tom and Will and Jack and their ma headed back up the crooked path to the cabin.

Feeling mighty hungry from a day's worth of excitement, the boys rushed into the cabin and sat down to eat. Jack's ma went into her kitchen . . . and came back out.

"Now, which one of you boys has got the sody sallyratus?"